LAZAR, THE GOOD DEED DOG

Giving Love and Respect to Our Elderly

written by Myrna Gelman Shanker

illustrations by Linda Robinson

IGI Press
A division of Lerner Publishing Group, Inc.
241 First Avenue North
Minneapolis, MN 55401 U.S.A.

Library of Congress Cataloging-in-Publication Data

Shanker, Myrna Gelman.
    Lazar, the good deed dog / written by Myrna Gelman Shanker ; illustrations by Linda Robinson.
        p.   cm.
    Summary: Illustrations and rhyming text introduce Lazar, a rescued Golden Retriever who spends his time visiting senior citizens at their residence. Includes facts about Lazar, ways to connect with seniors, and how to explain to children old age and the importance of helping others.
    ISBN 978–0–9829273–0–4
    [1. Stories in rhyme. 2. Golden retriever—Fiction. 3. Dogs—Fiction. 4. Old age—Fiction.] I. Robinson, Linda, ill. II. Title.
PZ8.3.S499Laz 2010
[E]—dc22   2010033183

Manufactured in the United States of America
2 – CG – 4/1/11

DEDICATION

This book is dedicated with love to my parents (of blessed memory), Ada and Gus Gelman. Their tender hearts, their good deeds, and the love and respect they showed to their children and parents shall always be remembered.

ACKNOWLEDGMENTS

To Lazar and all of the other sweet animals that connect with people in such a profound way. Words cannot express how much their cuddles, licks, and intuitive responses enrich the lives of the people they touch.

To my husband and children for their love and support of this and all other endeavors: Mickey, Wendy, Josh, and his wife, Tova.

To my sister Anita for her love and insight into this creative, animal-loving venture.

To Carol Rosenberg, Executive Director of Jewish Senior Life of Metropolitan Detroit, and to Barbra Giles, MSW, ACSW, Administrator of Fleischman Residence/Blumberg Plaza of Jewish Senior Life of Metropolitan Detroit, West Bloomfield, Michigan. Their belief in this project and contributions to its content were very important and extremely appreciated.

To The Alpern Life Enhancement Program. Thanks to this family's gift to Jewish Senior Life at the Fleischman Residence/Blumberg Plaza, Lazar and its residents have healthier, happier, more stimulating lives.

A portion of the proceeds of this book will benefit the quality of life for Jewish Senior Life of Metropolitan Detroit.

A NOTE TO PARENTS FROM THE AUTHOR

Lazar, The Good Deed Dog is based upon a real living situation. Lazar, a Golden Retriever Rescue Dog, lives at the Fleischman Residence/Blumberg Plaza, Jewish Senior Life of Metropolitan Detroit – a senior residence in West Bloomfield, Michigan. His presence there enhances the lives of those elders whose families and pets live elsewhere, thus eliminating the negative effects of loneliness, vulnerability, and boredom. The lives of both Lazar and our seniors emerge healthier and happier from this unique and positive relationship.

Lazar became my vehicle to encourage both parents and children alike to share time with our older adults, satisfy their needs, and also be enriched from their vast and varied experiences. How fascinating to hear what they have to say about life: their views on childhood, parenting, relationships, careers, and spiritual beliefs, too.

Our lives and the lives of our children have become so very busy. There are school activities, after-school activities, competitive sports, music lessons, dance lessons, tutorials, and other appointments to keep our children well-informed and stimulated. As parents, we want our kids to grow up to be happy, healthy, clever, and responsible.

It is also important for them to be other-directed: kind, compassionate, and interested in the lives of others. To give of themselves in a selfless, loving way... doing good just for the sake of making the world a better place. It is my hope that Lazar inspires each of us to do just that.

Myrna Gelman Shanker

"The world exists for the sake of kindness." ~Rashi

EXPLAINING OLD AGE TO CHILDREN

Even though our elders look older and can appear more frail, they are young people inside. They can identify with our lives, for they were young once, too.

Just as we have good days and bad, so do our older adults.

Aging is a part of living. One day we will grow old, too.

We can brighten the lives of our seniors and enhance their well-being by including animals, plants, and children in their lives.

We must celebrate the beauty within every person by being tender, loving, and compassionate.

Lazar is a big, kind dog
Who's joined a family:
His residence is Fleischman,
And his friends, the elderly.

Fleischman
Residence/
Blumberg Plaza

Lazar walks the hallways

And peeks in every room.

"Good morning, Mrs. Mandelbaum!"

"Hello there, Mr. Bloom!"

"How's it going, Harold?
Want to take a walk with me?
Think about it buddy...
Off to Room 2-2-0-3!"

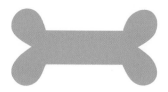

Our seniors are important
And need to know we care.

Lazar knows this all too well
And that's what he does there.

He's there for Mrs. Epstein
As they sit and watch TV.

She was once a teacher
And excels at JEOPARDY!!!

He's there for Mr. Cohen
As he plays his Rummi-Q.
And listens to his stories
About his childhood, too.

There for Mrs. Friedman

At her weekly wash and set.

She was in the movies.

A beauty still? You bet!

There for Mr. Lewis
Who knows how to dance and sing.

A Foxtrot or a Tango...
He can do most anything!

There for Dr. Solovitch
A long-time pediatrician.

Runny nose or earache?
Doctor "S" is on a mission!

There for Mrs. Eisenberg,

An artist and designer.

Lazar stops to see her work -

His portrait couldn't be finer!

There for Abie Besser
Who wears medals on his cap.
He served in the Army
And shows where on a map.

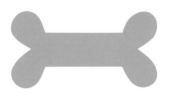

The Axis and its Allies
The Allies
Axis-occupied or Controlled
Vichy
Neutral States
Farthest Extent of German Advance in U.S.S.R.

ICELAND

UNION OF

SOVIET SOCIALIST

REPUBLICS

Archangel

GREAT BRITAIN

IRISH FREE STATE

HOLLAND

DENMARK

NORWAY

SWEDEN

FINLAND

Leningrad

ESTONIA

LATVIA

LITHUANIA

Memel

Smolensk

Moscow

Dunkirk

BELGIUM

Paris

GERMANY

SUDETANLAND

SAAR

CZECHIA

Danzig

EAST PRUSSIA

Warsaw

POLAND

Voronezh

Kiev

Stalingrad

FRANCE

Vichy

SWITZER LAND

AUSTRIA

SLOVAKIA

HUNGARY

Rostov

PORTUGAL

SPAIN

CROATIA

ITALY

SERBIA

RUMANIA

BULGARIA

CAUCASUS MTS.

ALBANIA

GREECE

TURKEY

PERSIA

CCO

ALGERIA

There for all the residents
Who eat at The Nosh Nook.

Lazar loves the strudel,
The corned beef and the cook!

It wasn't always cheerful
For Lazar... that's for sure.

Before he came to Fleischman
He was sad and insecure.

Scared about his future,
His home was on the streets.

He yearned for a new family,
Some petting and some treats.

One day he was rescued;
Lazar now lives happily
And dedicates his days to
Acts of Kindness... that's the key!

Do you know an elder

Who has a song to sing?

A story that needs telling?

A phone that longs to ring?

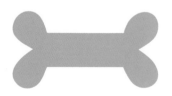

Listening to the many tales,
The lives they've lived - you'll see
These are the ones deserving of
Respect and dignity.

Pay a visit, make a call.

There's so much you can share.

It elevates the senior's life

Just knowing that you're there.

Sometimes we get all caught up

With texting or some blog.

So, take a tip from Lazar -

A mensch, a pal, and dog.

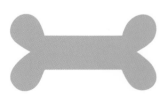

CONNECTING WITH A SENIOR FRIEND OR RELATIVE

Take time out of your busy schedule to share in the lives of a senior friend or family member.

Have a talk. Ask about childhood memories. Where did you grow up? Where did you go to school? What was your favorite subject or hobby? Who were your best friends?

Ask about being a young adult. For example – did you marry? Do you have children? Pets? How did you earn a living? Remember, too, it is important just to listen.

Talk about yourself. What are the things you like to do? Who are the people who mean the most to you? Share a story! Maybe tell a joke!

Play a board game or cards.

Prepare a simple recipe together, or just share a meal.

Play music. Sing. Dance.

Take a walk together. Make a bouquet of flowers.

Bring a pet to visit.

Hold a hand. Give a hug.

Be friendly, kind, and compassionate.

Provide the love and respect they are so deserving of, and experience the joy of having done so!

ABOUT LAZAR

 Lazar is a ten-year-old Golden Retriever who was rescued from an animal shelter in Flint, Michigan and brought to the Fleischman Residence/Blumberg Plaza, Jewish Senior Life of Metropolitan Detroit – a senior residence in West Bloomfield, Michigan.

Thanks to the generosity of The Alpern Life Enhancement Program, Lazar now dedicates his days to Acts of Kindness by visiting his fellow seniors and participating in their daily activities. Both Lazar and his resident friends feel happier, healthier, and more stimulated from this unique and tender relationship. Lazar enjoys taking walks, taking naps, and noshing on the many treats he receives from his appreciative companions.

ABOUT THE AUTHOR

Myrna Gelman Shanker was born and raised in the Metropolitan Detroit area and attended the University of Michigan. She also lived in Paris, London, and New York, and had careers in both teaching and advertising. Myrna loves a good time and a good rhyme. This is her first children's book.

ABOUT THE ILLUSTRATOR

Linda Robinson is still growing up close to where she was born in beautiful Michigan. She has illustrated twenty books and is the author of the novel *Chantepleuré*. Linda loved drawing Lazar and the folks that Lazar cares for. Like her father and brother, they need hugs and loving care every day.